BOTS

THE GOOD, THE BAD, AND THE COWBOTS

by Russ Bolts
illustrated by Jay Cooper

LITTLE SIMON
New York   London   Toronto   Sydney   New Delhi

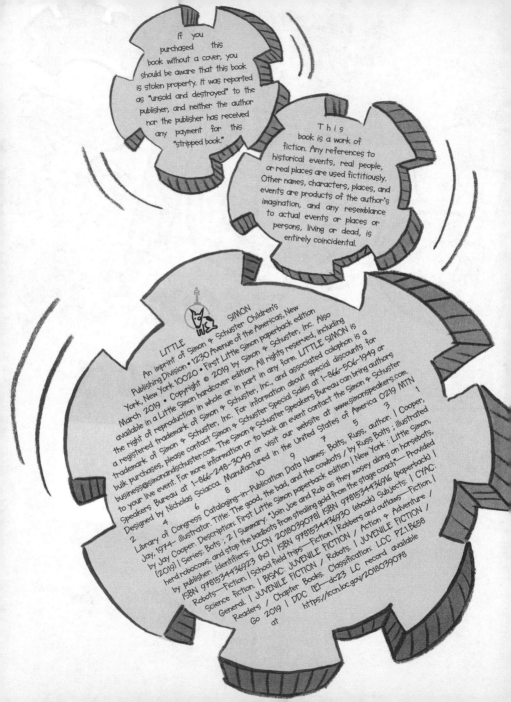

This book is a work of fiction. Any references to historical events, real people, or real places are used fictitiously. Other names, characters, places, and events are products of the author's imagination, and any resemblance to actual events or places or persons, living or dead, is entirely coincidental.

LITTLE SIMON
An imprint of Simon & Schuster Children's Publishing Division • 1230 Avenue of the Americas, New York, New York 10020 • First Little Simon paperback edition March 2019 • Copyright © 2019 by Simon & Schuster, Inc. Also available in a Little Simon hardcover edition. All rights reserved, including the right of reproduction in whole or in part in any form. LITTLE SIMON is a registered trademark of Simon & Schuster, Inc., and associated colophon is a trademark of Simon & Schuster, Inc. For information about special discounts for bulk purchases, please contact Simon & Schuster Special Sales at 1-866-506-1949 or business@simonandschuster.com. The Simon & Schuster Speakers Bureau can bring authors to your live event. For more information or to book an event contact the Simon & Schuster Speakers Bureau at 1-866-248-3049 or visit our website at www.simonspeakers.com. Designed by Nicholas Sciacca. Manufactured in the United States of America 0219 MTN
2   4   6   8   10   9   7   5   3   1
Library of Congress Cataloging-in-Publication Data Names: Bots, Russ, author. | Cooper, Jay, 1974- illustrator. Title: The good, the bad, and the cowbots / by Russ Bots ; illustrated by Jay Cooper. Description: First Little Simon paperback edition | New York : Little Simon, [2019] | Series: Bots ; 2 | Summary: "Join Joe and Rob as they mosey along on horsebots, herd robocows, and stop the badbots from stealing gold from the stage coach"—Provided by publisher. Identifiers: LCCN 2018039078| ISBN 9781534436916 (paperback) | ISBN 9781534436923 (hc) | ISBN 9781534436930 (eBook) Subjects: | CYAC: Robots—Fiction. | School field trips—Fiction. | Robbers and outlaws—Fiction. | Science fiction. | JUVENILE FICTION / Action & Adventure / General. | BISAC: JUVENILE FICTION / Robots. | JUVENILE FICTION / Readers / Chapter Books. Classification: LCC PZ7.B658 Go 2019 | DDC [E]—dc23 LC record available at https://lccn.loc.gov/2018039078

CONTENTS

CHAPTER 1

Hi-Ho, Robots!

Howdy, Earthling. To understand the story you are about to read, first you must remember how we met such strange and mysterious creatures as the Bots.

I am a scientist, like you. Unless you are not a scientist, in which case, I am a human, like you.

Hmm, unless you are not a human. Tell me, in your time, have dogs learned to read books yet?

Away!

Never mind. Where were we? Ah yes, Bots.

Many years ago, scientists created space cameras. They wanted to see what was at the end of the universe.

They blasted the space cameras out into space and then forgot about them.

Why did they forget? It's like forgetting your homework.

No matter how hard you try to remember, sometimes you forget.

Unless your dog ate it . . . or unless your dog read it.

YAWN.

We will get back to the reading dogs.

Soon the rockets reached the end of the universe and there was a planet! It was called Mecha Base One, and it was full of robots.

These robots—or Bots, as they like to be called—are very smart.

They built entire cities.

And spaceships.

And schools.

And even ice cream spaceships.

I know what you are thinking, but the spaceships are not made of ice cream. They only sell ice cream.

Out of this entire new world, these two young Bots found the space cameras.

Oh, and there is one other Bot to keep your eye on.

Tinny Bot

She might be a troublemaker.

Joe and Rob are two of the nicest, goofiest, and most kindhearted Bots in the universe. Our space cameras couldn't have found a more interesting duo.

For you non-scientists, "duo" is a word that means a pair of things. In this case, Joe and Rob are a pair of Bots, but they are also best friends.

Best friends do everything together.

They play Botball.

They play Botsketball.

In the winter, they even play Botsky.

But there's one thing every best friend must learn by themselves.

CHAPTER 2

Joe and Rob were on a field trip. Their class was studying how Bots used to live back in the olden days of the Wild West. Things were very different back then.

Bots had to ride horse-bots everywhere.

Stagecoach rockets delivered the mail.

Bots farmed the land to survive.

Small towns were built by good Bots.

But not all Bots in the Wild West were good.

It was Joe and Rob's teacher. Teachers do not think that dents are cool. In fact, teachers think that safe, educational lessons are cool.

If it were up to their teacher, Joe and Rob's class would have stayed at school and watched a video about the Wild West and horse-bot riding.

But luckily, Joe and Rob's class won a free trip to Robo-Ghost Town—the wildest, westernest Wild West place ever!

Joe and Rob were ready to become real cowbots!

CHAPTER 3

Howdy, Cou

Wait. What was the last thing the sheriff said? He said it really fast. Did he just say that he was going to teach the Bots how to rob a stagecoach? Maybe the camera signal is glitching. Let's rewind and listen to him again in slow motion.

A-N-D R-O-B A S-T-A-G-E-C-O-A-C-H.

Oh my. Teachers and students should definitely not like that.

Well, that was unexpected. At the very least the teacher should be upset about the spitting lesson. Hmm, let's see what happens next.

CHAPTER 4

The Moon Saloon

OK, PARTNERS. THIS HERE IS THE MOON SALOON. IT'S OUR FIRST STOP. YOU NEED TO KNOW A FEW THINGS BEFORE WE GO INSIDE.

FIRST, YOU'LL SEE A FANCY-LOOKING BUCKET BY THE DOOR.

THAT'S A SPITTOON.

REMEMBER TO ALWAYS SPIT IN THE SPITTOON WHEN YOU SEE A SPITTOON.

PLEASE DON'T SPIT ON THE GROUND. THAT'S RUDE AND GROSS.

SECOND, YOU'LL SEE A LOT OF COWBOTS PLAYING CARD GAMES INSIDE.

THEY LIKE TO PLAY GO ROBO-FISH.

JUST LEAVE THEM ALONE AND DON'T DISTURB THEM. THEY CAN BE A WILD BUNCH WHEN THEY GET EXCITED.

OH, AND THERE WILL BE A PIANO PLAYER INSIDE. HIS NAME IS HAL.
WHATEVER YOU DO, DO NOT TOUCH THE PIANO.
OLD HAL HATES WHEN ANYONE INTERRUPTS HIS SONGS.

But Joe wanted to be a real cowbot. Plus he wanted to impress Billy D. Error. So he was going to do whatever it took to fit in. Even if it meant spitting into every spittoon . . . which was a very bad idea.

41

EVERYBODY OUT!

CHAPTER 5

Robo-Rodeo

We have rodeos on Earth, but the rodeo in Robo-Ghost Town is a little different. For starters, everything is a robot.

Inside the arena, there were many cowbots trying to ride many different types of horse-bots and robo-bulls.

The Single Thruster Horse-bot

The Twin Thruster Horse-bot

The Super Snout Horse-bot

The Buckaroo Robo-Bull

The Octo-Rocket Robo-Bull

And of course, there was the most dangerous one of all . . .
Snuggles—the Pretty Little Pony Wony.

Hmm. Snuggles does not look dangerous.

And that's when things in Robo-Ghost Town got a little out of control.

57

CHAPTER 6

Robo-Rustlers

Now, before we see what happened to Joe and Snuggles, we should check in with Sheriff Billy D.

Hmm, usually sheriffs put up Wanted posters. They don't take them down.

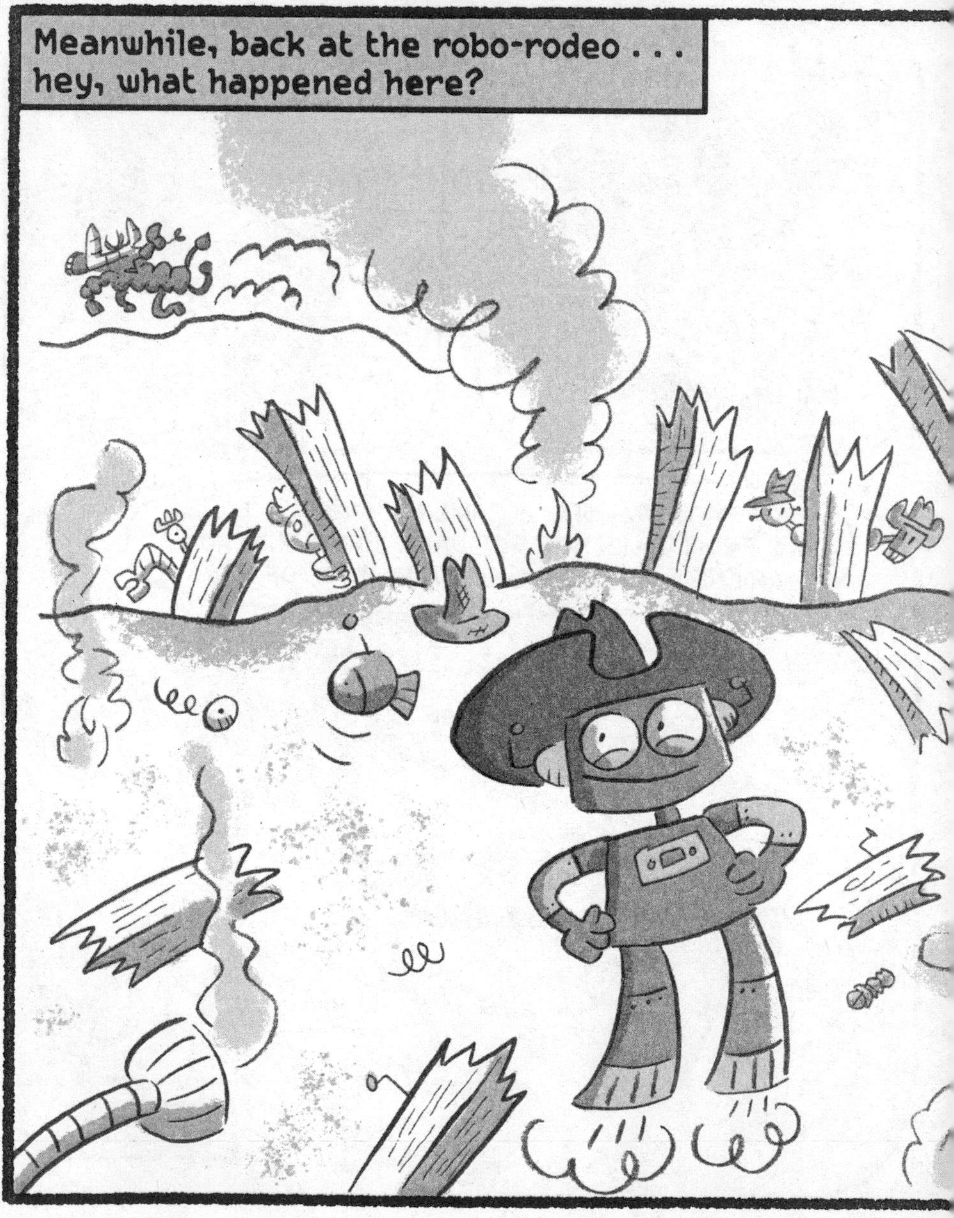
Meanwhile, back at the robo-rodeo . . . hey, what happened here?

Hold on. Let me find the footage of the robo-rodeo that we missed.

Everybody put your hands over your eyes. No peeking. You don't want any spoilers.

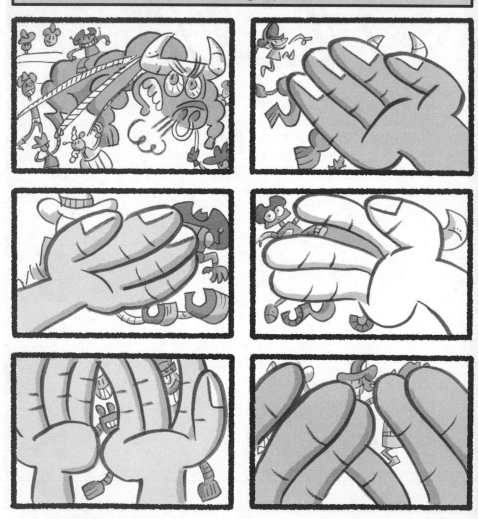

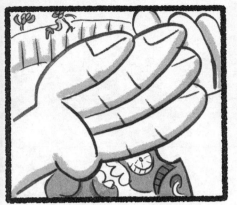

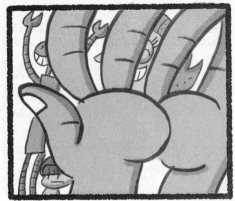

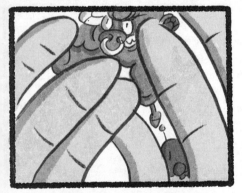

BAM!

Tinny Trouble

As Tinny dug through the saddle, Snuggles headed for a dark cave.

The cave wasn't empty. There was a crew of Bot Bandits waiting for their leader inside.

89

Evil Plan B

Without Snuggles for Billy D. to ride, the stagecoach would be safe.

Oh dear. I always forget about evil plan B!

95

Hmm, if the students climb onboard that crazy beast, then I'll eat my lab coat.

The stagecoach rocket flew past the robo-rodeo.

Cowbot Up

With our heroes holding on to the giant horse-bot, let's take a moment to look at Billy D.'s evil plan.

BILLY D. ERROR'S EVIL PLAN

STAGECOACH
$
LOTS OF GOLD
TRAIN →

TRACTER BEME

$

↑ SNUGGLES

SLOW 4 COACH

$

WOE! WOE!

THIS IZA ROBRY!

WAH!

YAHOO!!!

What about me?

U can't fit in picture! HA HA!

JALE

STUDENTS

↑ TEECHER

Wow. That IS an evil plan!

At least the plan won't work without Snuggles, right? I doubt that puzzle of horse-bot bits will hold together.

Oh no. I'll go back to eating my lab coat.

But there was a speed train in the distance. And it was slowing down!

No one can stop Billy D. Error now!

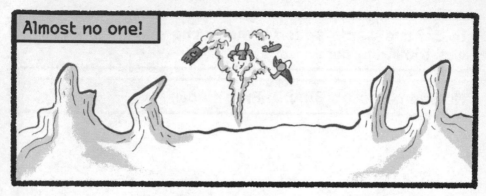

Almost no one!

CHAPTER 10

Robo-Horsing

When an object moves at a fast rate of speed, it creates a lot of energy.

And when a fast object connects with another object, it gives—or transfers—that energy to the new object.

There is a word for this: CRASH!

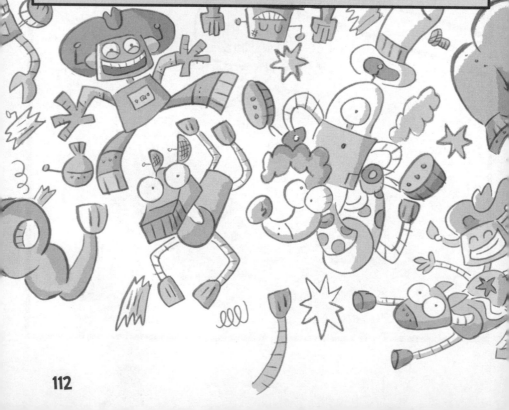

Around

115

As the Bot School ended their Robo-Ghost Town trip, Billy D. Error and his gang were in jail, the speed train was safe, and the town cheered on Joe and Rob with a hip-hip-hooray!

I would suggest you turn off the video now.
Old Hal is not going to like what happens next.

TUNE IN NEXT TIME FOR...

#3

BOTS

20,000 ROBOTS UNDER THE SEA

by **Russ Bolts** illustrated by **Jay Cooper**